Little Catholic Clubhouse

&
the True Meaning of Christmas

Written by
Mike and Sarah Zimmerman

Illustrated by
Sarah Zimmerman

It is more blessed to give
than to receive
- Acts 20:35

Nihil Obstat:

Rev. Jayd D. Neely
Censor Librorum

Imprimatur:

Most Rev. David R. Choby
Bishop of Nashville
5/17/17

"Oh boy! Grandma's Christmas present came today! I wonder what it is?" said Pete excitedly. Pete was always allowed to open Grandma's present early, so this was a treat.

"A sweater? Why would Grandma think I wanted a silly sweater when all I asked for was a bunch of toys? Yuck!" Pete yelled, as he held up the sweater with disgust, completely ignoring the Christmas card inside.

Pete's mom looked sad as she picked the card out of the box, opened it, and read it to Pete. She read, "Dear Pete, I love and miss you so much. I've made this sweater just for you. Merry Christmas, sweetie! Hugs, Grandma."

Pete's mom explained: "Pete, your grandma spent a lot of time making that sweater for you. You should be thankful that she gave you anything at all. Presents are not what Christmas is about. I don't think you understand what the true meaning of Christmas is."

Pete could see that his mother was upset, but he didn't understand why. He also didn't understand why his grandma would send him a sweater or what this *true meaning of Christmas* was about? He went to bed confused.

Pete's friends Marcus and Maria came running up to him at school the next day. "Hi Pete!" they greeted him. "Did you get the present from your grandma? What kind of toy did she send you?" they asked him. Embarrassed that he didn't get a toy, he told them what his mother had said; "The true meaning of Christmas is not about toys and presents".

Looking confused, Maria asks; "Then what *is* the true meaning of Christmas?" Pete didn't know what to say because he didn't know the answer. "It's uh...well you see..." he stammered, "Actually, I'm not sure, I just know it's not supposed to be about the toys." Now all three children were wondering about this *true meaning of Christmas.*

"It sounds like a question for the Little Catholic Clubhouse!" said Marcus excitedly. "You're right!" agreed Pete and Maria. All together they said; "A clubhouse meeting must be called to ask a question and get it solved." Then their club wristwatches sent out an emergency meeting alert.

They found their friends already waiting for them inside the clubhouse. "What's going on?" asked Lucas. "Why did you three call a meeting?" wondered Mattie. Pete explained; "We called a meeting to find out what the *true meaning of Christmas* is and why we celebrate it with presents. Do any of you know?" They all shook their heads "no". "Well, that's why we're here. Let's ask!" Pete shouted.

"Welcome, Little Catholics! How can I help you today?" asked the computer behind them. "Hello Father Q, we need to find out what the true meaning of Christmas is, can you help us?" asked Pete.
"Of course! As you all know, I could tell you kids the answer, but it's always more fun to show you! You guys know what to do,"
joked Father Q.

They all took their places on the platform and said the words that they knew would take them back in time. Together they shouted, "Father Q, please send us back in time so that we can see what we need to find. Together we can find the truth and act as God would want us to".

They were suddenly in a new place. It was a quiet night, and they were standing in the middle of a small town. At first, there was no one on the street. Then, they saw someone coming.

It was a man with a donkey. A lady was riding the donkey. They were knocking on doors and asking for a place to stay. No one had room for them. The man at the door of the Inn said that the only place he had was in the stable around back. They found the stable, and the family went in.

"Where are we?" Maria asked. "You are in the town of Bethlehem," Father Q answered on Maria's watch, "This is a very special place in our faith, and someone special is being born right now."

After awhile, the children entered the stable where the family was. "Who are they?" asked Mattie. "That's Mary and Joseph! And that baby must be Jesus!" exclaimed Lucas. The Little Catholics quietly watched Mary as she smiled at baby Jesus in her arms. The sheep and cattle laid down near Mary and Joseph to keep them warm.

After a little while, three kings arrived and came into the barn. "Those must be the three wise men!" Marcus said, "Look, they are bringing him presents!" The three wise men each took a turn laying a special present at the feet of Mary and baby Jesus.

"What are those?" Marcus asked. Marcus' watch beeped as Father Q chimed in again, "These are very expensive gifts. They are gold, frankincense, and myrrh. The gold is for Jesus because He is Christ, the King of Kings. The frankincense is to be used for prayer because Jesus teaches us to pray to God. And the myrrh is a burial spice because Jesus would die for our sins."

"Oh, that makes sense!" Lucas said, "They brought Him presents in honor of His birthday." "I guess this would be His very first birthday party then," giggled Marcus. "Actually, you're right," Father Q explained, "Because He is so special, we celebrate Jesus' birthday every year. It is what we celebrate on Christmas."

"It looks like you understand the meaning of Christmas!" Father Q said proudly, "I think it's time to come back to the Clubhouse."All of the Little Catholics gathered together and transported back to their own time.

"Is that why we give gifts on Christmas to those who are special to us?" Pete asked. All of the Little Catholics nodded their heads in agreement.

"Thank you, Father Q, for showing us why Christmas is so very special. Christmas is not about toys. We give gifts to those we love because they are special to us and special to Jesus too. No matter what the present is, it is given out of love," Pete declared. "I have to get home and talk to my mom."

Pete found his mom sitting at the kitchen table. "Mom, I think I understand what you meant about the true meaning of Christmas. Christmas is not about toys or presents. It's about showing people that they are special to you by giving gifts, just like the wise men gave gifts to baby Jesus," Pete said.

"Pete, you are absolutely right. I am so proud of you!" said Pete's mom smiling. "Mom, I'd like to call Grandma now and thank her for my sweater. I know she made it special for me, and it must have taken her a long time. She must love me a lot!" Pete exclaimed.

Points to ponder...

1) Why was Pete upset his Grandma sent him a sweater for Christmas?

2) Pete's mom told Pete he didn't understand the "meaning" of what?

3) What town did Father Q send the Little Catholics to? Who did they see there?

4) Why did Joseph & Mary have to sleep in a stable?

5) Who came to visit baby Jesus in the manger?

6) What three presents did the wise men bring Him? Why did they choose to give him these specific gifts?

7) Who's birthday do we celebrate every Christmas?

8) The wise men gave Jesus gifts because He was special to them. Who do you give gifts to, to show they are special to you and to celebrate Jesus being born?

9) Who does Pete call when he gets home? What does he want to say?

10) Is the true meaning of Christmas about toys or is it about giving gifts to people you love?

Meet the Characters

Hi! My name is <u>Pete</u>. I'm a 1st grader at St. Mary Magdalene's. I have one younger sister and we love to play soccer together. Another thing you should know about me, is that I love animals. My dog Pancake, is a Golden Retriever, and he is one of my best friends. When I grow up I want to a be a veterinarian so that I can help and work with animals everyday. Some of my favorites are:
<u>Favorite Saints:</u> St. Francis of Assisi, St. Sebastian, St. Anthony
<u>Favorite Food:</u> Pizza <u>Favorite Color:</u> Blue <u>Favorite Bible Story:</u> Noah and the Ark

Hola! My name is <u>Maria</u> and I am in the 1st grade at St. Mary Magdalene's. I am the youngest child in my family, with five older siblings. With six kids, a dog named Winnie and a cat named Poppy, our house is always buzzing with activity. I have a big family and I love every minute of it. I also love drawing and helping others. When I grow up I want to become a Religious Sister, so I can help others everyday. Some of my favorites are:
<u>Favorite Saints:</u> St. Bernadette, St. Theresa of Calcutta, St. Philomena
<u>Favorite Food:</u> Mac and Cheese <u>Favorite Color:</u> Teal <u>Favorite Bible Story:</u> The Good Samaritan

Hey everyone! My name is <u>Marcus</u> and I'm also a 1st grader at St. Mary Magdalene's. I have a younger brother and a cat named Snowflake. I love to learn, to read and I love anything to do with outer space. When I grow up I want to be a teacher so I can help others learn everyday. Some of my favorites are:
<u>Favorite Saints:</u> St.Patrick, St. Jude, St. Michael <u>Favorite Food:</u> Watermelon
<u>Favorite Color:</u> Green <u>Favorite Bible Story:</u> Jesus and the Beatitudes

Hello, my name is <u>Mattie</u>. I am a kindergartner at St. Mary Magdalene's. I love singing, baking and all things glittery. I have two bunnies named Rosie and Sparkles. I love baking them little treats with my mom. When I grow up I want to be a chef, so I can bake things for all the bunnies of the world, and maybe some people too. Some of my favorites are:
<u>Favorite Saints:</u> St. Theresa, St. Mary Magdalene, St. Cecilia
<u>Favorite Food:</u> Cake <u>Favorite Color:</u> Pink <u>Favorite Bible Story:</u> The Resurrection

Hi! My name is <u>Lucas</u>. I have two older sisters and a younger brother. While I'm one of the middle kids in my family, I'm the oldest member of the "Little Catholic Clubhouse". I love to swim and love to hang out with my talking parrot, Franklin. He makes me laugh. I also really love volunteering with my family. Helping others makes me happy. I want to be a Priest when I grow up. Some of my favorites are:

Favorite Saints: St. Nicholas, Padre Pio, St. Joan of Arc **Favorite Food:** Chicken Nuggets **Favorite Color:** Maroon **Favorite Bible Story:** Crossing the Red Sea

Hi! My name is <u>Johnny.</u> I'm a kindergartner at St. Mary Magdalene's. I have one younger sister and an older brother. We like to play video games together. I also love turtles (I have two pet ones) and being outside. One of my favorite things to do is to go fishing with my dad. When I grow up I want to be a scientist like him. Some of my favorites are:

Favorite Saints: St. Peter, St. Joseph, St. Christopher **Favorite Food:** Fish sticks **Favorite Color:** Yellow **Favorite Bible Story:** Jesus Feeds the Five Thousand

Hello! My name is <u>Father Q!</u> I am a priest and I mentor for the Little Catholic Clubhouse. While I live in Vatican City, they know I am only a quick call away. I enjoy helping the "Little Catholics" find the answers to their questions by guiding them, on our adventures, in the right direction. Through my own education and through scripture, I help the club solve their problems and figure out how to live the way Jesus would like. Some of my favorites are:

Favorite Saints: Pope St. John Paul II, St. John Vianney, St. Thomas Aquinas **Favorite Food:** Spaghetti **Favorite Color:** Orange **Favorite Bible Story:** Moses and the Ten Commandments

Little Catholic Clubhouse is proud to announce that we are teaming up with Our Lady of the Lake Catholic Church (OLOL) in Hendersonville, TN to help create hope for so many children in Haiti. Through the Parish Twinning Program of the Americas, OLOL has been paired up with St. Bertin Catholic Church in Petit Bourg de Port Margot, Haiti for the past 30 years and the two have formed such a special bond. Over the years, OLOL has been able to provide help to St. Bertin through financial aid, medical and dental care missions, sea container shipments, support in caring for the poor through the St Vincent de Paul Society and much more.

With continuous support from OLOL, St. Bertin has been able to educate thousands of students and together these two parishes have brightened futures, inspired dreams and created hope for so many countless individuals. Through funding, OLOL has helped St Bertin rebuild damaged and destroyed buildings from the 2010 earthquake while also adding additional classrooms to support the school's future growth, a future both communities want to see succeed. Through generous people and hard work, St. Bertin is achieving their goals and one man's vision is paving the way.

A man named Marc-Endy Saintil, once a former student of St. Bertin, had a dream...to earn a college degree, return to St. Bertin, and start a secondary school to give students the gift of life-changing education. In a country where only 5% of students advance to secondary school, his work was cut out for him but he prevailed. Today because of his determination and lots of prayers & support from OLOL, Marc-Endy's vision is now a reality.

For the first time ever, students at St. Bertin are able to continue their education beyond 6th grade, as 7th and 8th grades have been added at the new secondary school, under the supervision of their new principal, MARC-ENDY.
How amazing is that?

The story's far from over. As St. Bertin grows (and we hope it does) they will need more support, to maintain the current classes for their 650 students while at the same time adding new grades. We want to be part of this amazing story.

Here at Little Catholic Clubhouse, we believe that education is one of the best gifts any child can receive and we also want to foster a relationship where kids help other kids. How great a world that would be? We pledge to give 10% of all of the company's proceeds from book sales to St. Bertin. Every time someone buys a Little Catholic Clubhouse book they are helping a child in Haiti receive a Catholic education and giving them hope for a better future.

We hope you join us on this journey to support our dear brothers and sisters in Haiti and make their world a bit brighter. For more information, visit our web site.

CPSIA information can be obtained
at www.ICGtesting.com
Printed in the USA
BVOW05s1748301117

501578BV00022B/502/P